BACK FROM
THE GRAVE

ANNE SCHRAFF

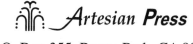

P.O. Box 355, Buena Park, CA 90621

STANDING TALL MYSTERY SERIES
MULTICULTURAL READERS
SET 3

Project Editor: Molly Mraz
Illustrator: Fujiko
Graphic Design: Tony Amaro
©2003 Artesian Press

Artesian **Press**

ISBN 1-58659-101-0

CONTENTS

Chapter 1

Ramone Fraser had just dropped off his girlfriend at her house. He was feeling great. Caline Bennett was the prettiest girl in the senior class at Drew High School. Ramone never thought she would go out with him, but she did. Tonight's date was super. At the door, Caline gave him a kiss and told him to call her again soon.

Ramone was driving a little too fast through the downtown streets. It was almost midnight, and the streets were pretty empty. A few bars were still open, including Sam's Bar on Seventeenth Street, near where Ramone lived. Ramone was humming to himself and still enjoying the pleasant smell of

Caline's perfume in his old car as he roared down Seventeenth Street.

Suddenly, there was a man in the street right in front of him. Ramone couldn't believe his eyes. It was as if the guy appeared out of nowhere. Ramone hit the brakes and the car skidded sideways.

"Oh man! Oh man!" Ramone cried. He was sure he was going to hit the guy, but somehow he missed him. His terror turned into rage.

He yelled out at the man, "Fool! Are you crazy or what? You almost got killed!"

The running man turned toward Ramone. He stood right under the glare of a streetlight. Ramone gasped in shock. The whole right side of the man's face looked melted. His right eye was gone. He was horribly disfigured.

The man disappeared into an alley, and Ramone sat there in the car for a few minutes. He felt numb. Slowly, the feeling began to return to his body. The guy looked like a monster from a horror movie, but he was a human being. And Ramone had almost killed him. It all happened so fast. Ramone half-believed it hadn't happened at all. It was like a nightmare.

Maybe the guy was wearing a mask, Ramone thought as he slowly drove on. *What was he doing running into the middle of the street?* Now that Ramone thought about it, the guy must have been running from Sam's Bar. Ramone turned around in the middle of the street and drove back to the bar. He wanted to ask Sam Davis, the bartender, if he knew anything about the scarred man and what he was running from. Ramone was seventeen, almost eighteen. He wasn't supposed to go into a bar, but he didn't think it was wrong to walk in just to talk to Mr. Davis. He had known him for years.

As Ramone got close to the bar, he

heard the jukebox playing. Sam ran an old time bar. His customers were older men. He had an old-fashioned jukebox and posters of John Wayne and other long-dead movie stars on the walls.

Ramone opened the door and looked toward the bar. He didn't see Sam. "Hey, anybody home?" he shouted. It was dark inside the place. The jukebox was blaring. A girl with a sweet voice was singing,

"I thought you loved me, baby,
Goes to show that I'm a fool,
You lied and you cheated,
You broke every rule . . ."

"Mr. Davis?" Ramone called out. "Anybody here?"

Ramone walked closer to the bar. He was getting an uneasy feeling.

Then Ramone saw Sam behind the bar. He was lying on the floor. Blood formed a pool around his head. His eyes were open, but he couldn't see through them anymore.

He was dead. Sam Davis was dead.

Ramone was horrified. He followed his instincts. He ran back to his car and grabbed his cell phone. He called 9-1-1 and told the police about Sam. Ramone did not give his own name. He was scared. Last summer, Ramone spent four months in the youth authority camp for drug dealing. He had a record. He didn't want to risk being linked to a murder!

Ramone drove home through the darkness. His heart pounded and he had a headache that made it almost impossible for him to see.

Chapter 2

When Ramone got home, his father was still up. He was working on his computer. Mom and Ramone's two little sisters had gone to bed.

"Hey, Ramone," Dad said, "did you have a good time tonight?"

"Uh, yeah," Ramone said. He and his dad were close, but that good relationship almost ended last summer. Dad was really disappointed when Ramone got into trouble, but Dad was even more upset that Ramone had lied to him. The truth came out only when the police came to the house to talk to Ramone. Now Ramone had the feeling that Dad didn't trust him anymore, so he decided not to mention what happened tonight. Dad might think Ramone wasn't telling the whole truth, like before. So Ramone just went to bed.

Last spring, Ramone and his best friend, Larry Nash, started hanging out with an older boy who'd dropped out of Drew High two years ago. His name was Spyder Purvis. He drove a flashy car and wore gold chains around his neck. He always seemed to have pretty girls around him, girls like Courtney Lewis and Tomika Haines.

Pretty soon, Ramone and Larry wanted to know why Spyder always had so much money. They found out that Spyder was dealing drugs. The boys started to deal drugs for Spyder. Spyder was smart. When the police found out about the drugs, Larry and Ramone got caught, but Spyder did not. Both boys had no criminal records up to then, so they had to spend only four months in the youth authority camp.

It was a very tough time in Ramone's

life. His parents grounded him for months. Even now they watched him all the time. Dad warned Ramone that he would be in big trouble if he ever went near Spyder again. Larry's parents weren't as strict. Although Larry came back to Drew High, he sometimes had a hamburger with Spyder.

Ramone didn't want anything more to do with judges and lockups. When someone brought drugs to a party, Ramone left. Larry wasn't dealing anymore, but he still used drugs sometimes. So Ramone ended his friendship with him.

The morning after he found Sam dead, Ramone saw a small group of girls crying together when he arrived at Drew High. One of the girls was sobbing while the others tried to comfort her. When Ramone got closer, he realized they were talking about Sam Davis' death. The girls were friends of Leeza Davis, Sam's daughter.

"He died right there on the floor," one of the girls said.

Another girl said, "The police have no idea who did it."

Ramone went to the edge of the crowd, and a girl named Kim turned to him. "Ramone, did you hear? Leeza's dad got killed last night."

Leeza wasn't a friend of Ramone's, but he knew her. She was a junior. She was a nice, sweet girl who got straight A's.

"That's terrible," Ramone said.

"Yeah," Kim said. "I guess somebody came in to rob him and maybe he put up a fight or something."

Ramone felt terrible. He hadn't even told the police about the scarred man running from the direction of the bar. All he said in the 9-1-1 call he made was that a man was dead at Sam's Bar. Ramone probably could identify the murderer, and he was keeping quiet about it.

"Sam Davis was a good man," Kim said. "It's so awful that he died like that!"

"Yeah," Ramone said. Then he hurried off to his first class.

All through math and history class, Ramone thought about what happened last night. He kept seeing the awful-looking man running in front of his car. Ramone was probably the only person who saw the guy—the only witness.

But Ramone did not want to admit to the police that he was on Seventeenth Street when Sam Davis was killed. What if the police thought Ramone did it? What if they thought that Ramone Fraser needed some money, and he went in and tried to get it from Sam? Then, when the robbery didn't work out, he panicked and shot Sam. After all, Ramone had a record. He wasn't a good kid who never got in trouble with the police.

Ramone could imagine describing

the guy to the police. It didn't even make sense. He was like a monster out of a horror movie. No, the police would probably think that Ramone was trying to blame his crime on someone else.

Chapter 3

Ramone tried to convince himself that the scarred man wasn't even the murderer. He was probably just a guy who wanted a drink and went into Sam's Bar. When he found the dead man, he ran, just like Ramone did. If Ramone went to the police with his description, he'd probably just be getting an innocent man in trouble.

That thought made Ramone feel better—not quite so guilty. It eased his guilt. He didn't know who shot Leeza's father. Why make trouble for some poor man who already had enough to deal with, looking the way he did?

Ramone started to think about other things. On Saturday, he was double dating with Larry and his girlfriend. It would be the first time Ramone really went anywhere with Larry since last summer. Larry got four great tickets to a rhythm and blues concert. He gave Ramone two tickets, one for himself and one for Caline. Ramone figured Larry still felt bad because he was the one who introduced Ramone to Spyder Purvis.

As Ramone drove home from school, he saw Spyder standing on the corner with another guy.

"Hey, man, got a minute?" Spyder yelled. The traffic light turned red, stopping Ramone at the corner.

"I'm running late," Ramone said coldly.

There weren't any cars behind Ramone, so Spyder came over and leaned in the window.

"The light turned green," Ramone said.

"What's your rush?" Spyder said. "Hey, you look pitiful, my man. Old clothes. A haircut like your grandfather. And how do you plan to get any attention from the ladies in this old car?"

"I'm doing fine," Ramone said. "Gotta go."

"Hey, that's no way to treat a friend," Spyder said.

"I'll give it to you straight, man," Ramone said. "My dad says if I have anything more to do with you, he's going to punish me like never before. To tell the plain truth, those four months in the mountains made me never want to do anything with you again."

"Man," Spyder said, "I don't think I've ever seen a boy turn into a chicken right before my very own eyes—until now."

"Got to go," Ramone said. As he drove away, he felt something hit the back of the car. It was a rock.

Spyder was looking for someone to do the dirty work in one of his schemes again. Hanging out with Spyder was like having a ticket to prison.

When Ramone walked into his family's apartment, he smelled steak. Dad was frying steaks, and Mom was tossing a salad. Ramone had a good family. He loved them. Remembering last summer, he couldn't believe he had been such a fool.

Ramone's sisters were on the floor putting together a big jigsaw puzzle. Ten-year-old Denyn jumped up when she saw Ramone.

"Ramone! Did you hear? Mr. Davis got killed last night. He was shot! Poor Mr. Davis!" she said.

Mr. Davis coached the girl's pony league baseball games. He did a lot for the community.

Ayanna joined in. "Everybody is talking about it at school. They're saying maybe a gang member did it," she said.

"I heard about it," Ramone said.

"It's so awful," Mom said, "when a

good, hard-working man like that is killed." She tossed the salad as she spoke. "We took some casseroles over to the family. There's not much else we can do. So many lives are torn apart. Mr. Davis has that teenaged girl and three grown children. He was a father and a grandfather. I hope the police find who did it!"'

Chapter 4

When Ramone went to bed that night, he still felt terribly guilty. He kept seeing the awful face of that man. What if he killed Mr. Davis? Now he was getting away with it, because Ramone wouldn't go to the police.

Ramone tossed and turned and couldn't sleep. Finally, he got out of bed and wandered around the dark house. He went to the kitchen to fix himself some warm milk. Ramone heard that warm milk sometimes helped people sleep. He tried not to make any noise. He didn't want to wake the rest of the family.

As Ramone sat at the kitchen table drinking the milk, he heard noises outside. He had an uneasy feeling in the pit of his stomach. The noises might just be cats or the wind, but still . . .

Ramone went to the window and opened the curtains a little. Then he gasped. The man he had almost hit with his car was outside, trying to look in Ramone's window! The man with the scarred face and missing eye was only a few feet away!

Ramone jumped back from the window. When he got the courage to look again, the guy was gone.

What was he doing here?

The man somehow tracked Ramone to his apartment. Maybe he took Ramone's car license plate number and did it that way. Surely he knew that Ramone was a witness to his running from the murder scene. Maybe he was planning to make sure the witness wound up dead!

Ramone broke out into a cold sweat. He had no choice now. He had to go to the police. The guy who probably killed Sam Davis was right here at his home. He was a threat to Ramone and his family. There was a violent monster out there in the darkness, and Ramone had to do something.

In the morning, Ramone told his parents what happened at Sam's bar. "I'm sorry I didn't tell you guys sooner," he said.

"I'm really disappointed in you, boy," Dad said. "I thought we were going to be open and honest with each other. You kept important information to yourself, Ramone. The police have lost valuable time, and that's your fault."'

"I'm sorry, Dad," Ramone said. "I just got so scared. I mean, I was afraid that if I went to the police, they'd think I killed Mr. Davis. You know, after the trouble last year. The police know I have a record."

Dad drove Ramone to the police

station. Ramone was taken into a small, cluttered room where Sergeant Tanner sat. He was a weary-looking man. He listened to Ramone's story and took some notes. Then he asked, "Did you actually see him run from the bar?"

"No," Ramone said, "but he was coming from that direction, and the bar was the only thing open on that side of the street. He had to be coming from there."

"You got a good look at him?" Sgt. Tanner asked.

"Yeah, I sure did. He turned and looked at me right after I almost hit him with my car. He's a horrible-looking guy. I guess what really scared me was that he was outside our apartment last night, like he knows that I saw him, and now he's after me," Ramone said.

Tanner called a police artist into the room. Ramone described the man he saw, and she started to draw a picture. As Ramone described more of the man's appearance, Sgt. Tanner frowned. He seemed angry. "Boy, are you making this up?" he demanded.

"What? No, of course not," Ramone said.

Sgt. Tanner left the room for a moment. He returned with a police photo of a criminal named Artie Porter. "Is this the guy?" he asked. He showed the picture to Ramone.

Ramone stared in shock at the photo. "Yeah! That's him!"

"There's just one problem," Sgt. Tanner said. "This guy died six months ago. Are you trying to tell me that he's back from the grave?" There was bitter sarcasm in the officer's voice.

Chapter 5

"But that's impossible!" Ramone cried.

"Look, boy," Sgt. Tanner said, "we're pretty busy around here. Right now we're trying to solve a murder and a couple of armed robberies and assaults. We don't have time for games. Artie Porter was a gangster celebrity. His picture was in all the papers when he died. He'd been in a fire, and he looked pretty bad. No doubt you saw his picture, and now you think it's funny to come in here and tell us you saw a dead guy running from the bar."

Ramone rocked back in his chair, shocked. "I swear that's the guy I saw outside the bar, and at my window last night. I can't explain it, but—"

Sgt. Tanner turned to another police officer. "Get this kid out of here before I lose my temper," he said. "Or before I arrest him for lying to the police!"'

As they headed home, Ramone asked his father, "You believe me, don't you, Dad?"

"I know you wouldn't lie about something this serious, Ramone. But if the guy died six months ago . . . Maybe you didn't get a good enough look at the man outside the bar, and you just imagined that he looked like Artie Porter," Dad said.

"I'm telling you, I saw that guy!" Ramone said.

"I remember an article about Artie Porter in the paper with his obituary," Dad said. "It said he was a murderer for the local organized crime family. The police could never prove that. They finally got him for cheating on his income tax."

"Right before he was arrested, he was in a terrible fire. The police suspected it was arson. Porter had plenty of enemies. One of them planned to burn him up, I guess. Porter was in the federal prison for ten years. He got out only a couple of years ago. The paper said he was a hermit—lived all alone somewhere. He was ashamed to go out in public. Then he died of a heart attack."

"Let's go down to the library, Dad," Ramone said. "We can dig out the picture of Porter and the article. I want to see it again. I want to make sure it was the guy I saw."

They went to the downtown library's newspaper reading room. Ramone brought up the article about Porter's death on a computer and printed it. He stared at the picture for a few minutes and then said, "Dad, that is him. I'm totally sure. I thought maybe I looked too fast at the photo in the police station.

I thought maybe I made a mistake. But this is the guy I saw running on Seventeenth Street the night Mr. Davis was killed."

"Ramone," Dad said as they left the library, "do you really believe the man has returned from the grave?"

"I don't know what to think. I didn't see that newspaper article when it was printed before. This is the first time I have seen it. You know I hardly ever read the paper, except for the sports section. How would I know what he looked like if I hadn't seen him?" Ramone said.

At home in his room, Ramone read the article over and over. It described Porter's miserable life. He grew up poor and then joined a local crime family. He worked his way up quickly. He started killing people for the crime boss. He was good at it, and pretty soon he was a celebrity himself. He went to famous nightclubs in Los Angeles and hung out with the movie and TV stars. The newspaper printed a photo of Porter before the fire. He was a handsome man. He looked good enough to be a movie star himself.

But the fire changed all that. Artie Porter's life completely fell apart. He was disfigured by the fire, then arrested and sent to prison. When he got out, he couldn't face the world—not the way he looked. He had been a proud man. He couldn't stand to have people look at him and turn away.

Maybe Porter faked his own death, Ramone thought. *Maybe he wanted to drop out of sight and hide.*

Chapter 6

As he drove to school the next day,
Ramone thought about Sam Davis. He
used to give Thanksgiving turkeys to the
poor families in the neighborhood. He
made Christmas stockings for the needy
children. He stuffed them with toys,
candy, and gold coins with the picture
of the Indian Princess Sacagawea on
them. Each of the coins was worth a
dollar, but they were more special than
paper dollars would have been. He kept
a big jar full of them.

Sam Davis was a good guy. He
deserved better than a bullet.

Ramone had lunch with Caline that
day. He told her everything that
happened.

"And the police wouldn't believe you?" Caline asked.

"No, because the guy I identified was dead!" Ramone groaned.

"Ramone! And he was outside your window?" Caline cried. "Maybe he's an evil spirit! A ghost!"

"No," Ramone said. "He was a real guy. As real as you and me. And I think he's out to shut me up."

"You've got to be so careful! Keep all your doors and windows locked," Caline said. "Call the police right away if you see him again."

Ramone figured that was good advice. But what about tonight when he went to work at the taco stand? Usually Ramone was all alone when he closed up around eleven-thirty. What if the scarred man showed up then?

Ramone stuck his cell phone in his pocket as he headed for work in the late afternoon. If there was any sign of trouble, he planned to hit the 9-1-1 buttons fast.

The taco stand was busy until about ten o'clock. Then there were fewer customers. A few couples showed up for the bargain tacos––three for the usual price of one, and a soft drink, too. But after that, there were only stragglers.

"Hey, man," a familiar voice called out in the darkness. "Still making pennies in this greasy joint, huh?"

"Yeah, Spyder," Ramone said. Ramone did not want to see Spyder tonight, but at least it wasn't the scarred man.

"You are such a fool," Spyder said. "I'm working on a couple of sweet deals, and you could be a part of them." He reached into his wallet and pulled out a thick pile of cash. He had twenties, fifties, and hundred-dollar bills.

Then some coins fell out of the wallet—gold dollars with Sacagawea's picture on them. They clattered on the floor of the taco stand, and Spyder stooped to pick them up.

"Where'd those come from?" Ramone asked.

"Some guy gave them to me," Spyder said. "Pretty, huh? She was some good-looking lady, this princess."

Ramone made the tacos Spyder ordered, and Spyder sat on the stool as he ate them. He gobbled them down, one after the other with big gulps of soda.

Ramone wondered if Spyder got the coins from Sam. Maybe the murderer dropped them in the street and Spyder picked them up.

"What do you hear about the killing at Sam's Bar?" Ramone asked.

"Probably some old loser getting even with the bartender. A lot of crazy old men hang around in there. They sit in there and drink all night," Spyder said.

"Did you hear that for sure or are you just making it up?" Ramone asked.

Spyder shrugged. "That's what I hear, man," he said.

Ramone decided to tell Spyder what he had seen to get his reaction. Spyder listened carefully. Then he asked, "Are you serious?"

"Yeah. This scarred guy ran in front of my car. I almost hit him. It was really wild. The whole side of his face looked like it was melted. And he didn't have a right eye. He looked like somebody out of a horror show. And then he showed up outside my window, like he was looking for me," Ramone said.

"Is your life insurance paid up?" Spyder asked.

Chapter 7

"I remember seeing Artie Porter's picture in the paper when he died," Spyder said. "He used to live around here. In the old days he was a paid killer. He had lots of money, but he wasn't smart. You hear what I'm saying? The man was a fool. He got caught." Spyder finished his tacos. "You sure you want to stay here, man? There's a whole other world out there, and it's green—like money," he said.

"I'm as sure that I don't want to join you as I'm sure that the sun sets in the west," Ramone said. He was still thinking about the Sacagawea dollars Spyder had. "Who'd you say gave you those gold dollars?"

"I didn't say," Spyder said with a sneer. He got up and walked out of the taco place. He turned once and looked back. His lips formed the word *fool*.

Customers thinned out to almost none. Ramone played some music on the radio. Then, around eleven-fifteen, he started to close up. There was no sense in keeping the lights on if nobody was showing up. A thick fog drifted in from the bay and wrapped itself around the buildings and the few parked cars. Everything looked spooky, and Ramone hurried to clean up and get out of there. When he finally locked up, he looked around to make sure nobody was hiding out on the street.

Ramone hurried toward his car, which was parked around the corner. The boss didn't want the employees parking in the taco stand lot and taking up spaces the customers needed.

Ramone got to his car and was about to put the key in the door when something sharp jabbed him in the back. He didn't think he was cut, but he knew he'd been jabbed by the pointed end of a knife.

The guy had come out of nowhere. He must have been hiding in the foggy darkness.

"Don't turn," a raspy voice commanded. "Just look straight ahead, kid. I got a sharp blade at your backbone!"'

Ramone felt his arms and legs go numb. He hadn't seen the guy behind him, but he knew who he was. It had to be him—the scarred man who'd run in front of him that night. "Look, I don't know what you want, Mister," Ramone stammered.

"Get down on the ground!" the angry voice ordered.

Ramone got down on his hands and knees. "I don't know what you want. I swear I didn't see anything the other night," Ramone lied.

Ramone was sure it was the scarred man. He must be here because he thought Ramone could identify him as a murderer and send him back to prison. And this time, Artie Porter would never get out. He had killed again—and this time, a good man died.

The man gave Ramone a hard shove and Ramone landed in the dirt. He felt the knife at the back of his neck now.

"You were revving your motor good that night," he said. He pressed the tip of the knife against Ramone's neck. "What was your big hurry?"

Ramone was breathing so hard that his voice came in gasps. Now he knew for sure this was the scarred man with the missing right eye. If there was any doubt, it was gone now. "I . . . I don't know what you mean," he said.

"What do you think I mean?" the man growled. His voice sounded evil. This was a man without a conscience— a man who could kill someone at noon

and enjoy a great meal that same night.
And he had a knife at Ramone's neck!

Chapter 8

"I was going home from a date," Ramone said. "I was just in a good mood. The streets were empty, so I leaned on the gas pedal. That's all."

"Liar!" the man hissed. He pressed the tip of the knife hard against Ramone's neck. "You were running scared. You almost killed me. What were you running away from? Did you and your friends rob the bar? The deal went bad, and you had to kill the little man behind the bar? Is that what happened?"

Ramone felt dizzy. All this time, he was sure the scarred man had killed Mr. Davis and was running from the scene of his crime. But this guy thought

Ramone was the killer and that he was running from the crime that night. Everything was turning upside down in Ramone's head. "I never robbed Mr. Davis," Ramone said. "I don't even have a gun."

"How did you know a gun killed him, then?" the scarred man asked.

"After I almost hit you, I turned around and went to the bar. I knew Mr. Davis. I thought he could tell me who you were," Ramone said. "I went in and saw Mr. Davis on the floor. I could tell he'd been shot, so I called 9-1-1 and got out of there."

The man didn't say anything for a few seconds. He seemed to be thinking about what Ramone said. Ramone wondered if he'd get out of there alive. He was dealing with a man who killed for a living. How could he expect to survive?

"A young guy killed Sam Davis," the man said slowly. "I always went in there late, when nobody was around. Sam would sell me a drink, and we'd sit and talk. Sam was a funny guy. He could look at me and talk to me and not turn away. He didn't care how people looked." There was a strange softness to the man's voice now. He almost sounded like a decent human being. Ramone's father once told him that there was a little good in even the worst of men, and a little bad in the best of men. Maybe that was true.

The man continued. "That night when I went in, Sam was already shot. He knew he was dying. He looked at me and gasped out a few words. He said a kid wearing a scarf over his face robbed him. The scarf slipped. Sam saw the guy's face and he got shot because of that. It was a young guy . . . like you." His voice was filled with hate.

"It wasn't me," Ramone whispered.

"I ran out of the bar. I thought I'd see the guy running away. All I saw was you. You, speeding in your car like you wanted to get away real fast," the man said.

"But I didn't do it," Ramone said.

The man pulled back the knife a bit. "You're not free yet, kid. If you killed Sam, you'll pay for it. I don't mean the police, either. I'll take care of you myself. Don't feel safe. Not for a minute. You won't escape me. I'll be in the shadows somewhere when you least expect it," he said. Suddenly, the knife was gone from the back of Ramone's neck. When he found the courage to turn and look, the man was gone, too.

Ramone was shaking as he stood up. He had somehow put enough doubt in the man's mind to spare his life, for now.

Ramone's legs felt too weak to support him. They felt like cooked spaghetti. Ramone dropped his keys twice before he got the car door open. He climbed behind the wheel, turned the ignition, and the car began to move.

Ramone couldn't believe he was still alive.

But for how long?

Chapter 9

The next afternoon after school, Ramone drove to Sam Davis' house, where his widow and daughter Leeza lived. Ramone had been there before. The last time was for the reception after Sam's funeral.

Leeza wasn't home. Ramone was glad because he wanted to talk to Mrs. Davis alone.

"Oh, Ramone," she said when she opened the door. "Thank your mother for those wonderful casseroles. And thank you all for all the hugs. I need them." The woman's eyes were red and swollen from crying.

"Mrs. Davis, I hate to bother you, but can I talk to you for a minute?"

Ramone asked.

"Sure, come in," she said. She led Ramone into the living room.

"The police haven't found the guy who killed your husband yet," Ramone said. "I'm trying to help them."

Mrs. Davis nodded. "I hope they catch him before he hurts somebody else. Sam was a good man. He was just about my whole life. We were going to get a motor home and travel when Leeza goes away to college. We had so many plans." Tears ran down her cheeks.

"I was driving past the bar the night it happened, and this man . . . this scarred man with one eye came running from that side of the street," Ramone said.

Mrs. Davis nodded immediately. "Rocky. That was Rocky. He lives in a room near the bar. He was burned in a terrible fire. Sam was one of the few people he'd show himself to. Rocky doesn't go out in public. He came to the funeral, but he wore a hat and a big coat with the collar up so you couldn't see his face. He stayed in the back. Sam was Rocky's only friend," she said. "Rocky told me about being there when Sam died. He came right after Sam was shot."

"What is Rocky's real name?" Ramone asked.

The woman looked at him. Ramone could tell that she knew, but she didn't want to talk about it. "Rocky is good enough," she said.

"His name is Artie Porter, isn't it?" Ramone asked.

Mrs. Davis sighed. "Sam told me Rocky wasn't always a good man, but he was trying to change. Sam didn't judge people. He always gave folks a chance. They say this Artie Porter died some time ago. Maybe he did, and maybe he didn't. But Rocky liked to think he did. Rocky wanted it like that," Mrs. Davis said.

Ramone was pretty sure he now knew what happened. Porter faked his own death. He wanted to start over as somebody else. Maybe enemies were after him. Maybe he just didn't want some reporter to find him, take his picture, and write some story for the newspaper.

So he faked his own death and became Rocky.

Mrs. Davis spoke in a soft and sad voice. "Rocky said my husband told him a young man had shot him. Sam saw his face, so the young man thought he had to kill my husband. It's hard to believe anyone could be so heartless."

Ramone remembered the gold coins Spyder had. Maybe he scooped them up from the bar before he left the dying man.

"Thanks for talking to me," Ramone said. "I'm really sorry about your husband. He was a good guy. Everybody liked him."

"I know. Everyone has been so kind to me. They're repaying the kindness Sam showed. I'll be all right. I have children and grandchildren. I have friends. I'll be all right," Mrs. Davis said before she started to cry again.

Ramone hurried from the house. He decided to find Courtney Lewis, Spyder's girlfriend.

Chapter 10

Courtney Lewis was sitting on her front porch with another girl, Tomika Haines. Ramone walked up and gave them a friendly smile. He didn't want to come right out and say he was looking for evidence linking Spyder to Sam Davis's murder.

"Hi, Courtney. Hi, Tomika," Ramone said. Tomika was Larry's date when Ramone and Caline went to the rhythm and blues concert with them.

"Hi," Courtney said. She was a beautiful girl, but Ramone thought she was stupid. She dropped out of Drew High School in her sophomore year to have more time to hang out with Spyder.

"That was a really amazing concert

the other night, wasn't it, Ramone?"
Tomika said.

"Sure was," Ramone said. "Man, it's been a weird week for me. I was right there on Seventeenth Street the night Mr. Davis was shot."

"No way!" Courtney said. "For real?"

"Yeah, I even saw the guy dead," Ramone said.

"Get outta here!" Courtney cried. "Are you serious?"

"Yeah," Ramone said. He tried to seem very cool and unconcerned. "The police don't know I was there. Like I'd tell them!" Ramone laughed.

"You didn't kill him, did you?" Tomika asked, her eyes wide.

"Nah," Ramone said, like it was no big deal.

"But you saw him, huh?" Tomika asked. "Was it all really gross?"

"You better believe it," Ramone said. "Blood all over."

"Ewwww," Courtney said with a shudder.

"The reason I came over," Ramone said, casually changing the subject. "I wanted to give Caline some of these gold dollars—you know, the ones with Sacagawea on them. Caline really likes them, and the other day Spyder had some. I was wondering if he would sell me some."

"How many do you need?" Courtney asked.

"Well, see, Caline's eighteenth birthday is coming up, and I was thinking I'd give her eighteen of them," Ramone said.

"I don't think Spyder has that many," Courtney said. "He said a guy just gave him a couple."

"Larry has a bunch of them," Tomika said. "I saw them in a big old jar."

"Oh yeah?" Ramone asked. His heart was pounding. He was fighting to stay calm and cool. "I never knew

Larry was a coin collector."

"No, he's not," Tomika said. "He just got these coins the other day. He didn't tell me where. But I bet he'd sell you some. Larry is always ready to make a deal."

Courtney laughed. "He's been making a lot of deals lately. Spyder's got a lot of money, but last week when he and Larry were comparing their wallets, Larry had even more. Spyder was kidding him. He said Larry is into some kind of business on the side," she said.

Ramone walked back to his car. He sat there a few minutes. Ramone didn't like telling on people. But this was murder, the murder of a good man. So he dialed 9-1-1 and told the police that they might want to question Larry about the murder of Sam Davis.

By the end of the day, seventeen hundred dollars in cash, two hundred dollars in gold Sacagawea coins, and

Sam Davis' expensive watch were found in Larry's home. Larry was arrested for robbery and murder.

Ramone felt sad. He used to think that he and Larry had both escaped the evil spider's web spun by Spyder Purvis. Now he knew that he alone had escaped.